# TV St★r

## Book 1

Rebecca Parkinson

Day One

Dedication
For Edward—the original Archie! Thank
you for always making us laugh!

# CONTENTS

# SCHOOL AGAIN!

**A**rchibald Edwards gazed at his reflection in the full-length mirror.

"Year four," he whispered, stretching his neck and spiking up his gelled, blond hair to make himself look taller.

"Well, Archie," he announced proudly, "you certainly look very handsome."

He shrugged his shoulders and pulled a funny face at himself.

"Handsome, but heading towards the worst day of your life," he added sadly.

His mum's frightening words rang in his head.

"When you're in year four, Archie, you will have to be grown-up. You must change your behaviour, work hard and do lots of homework!"

"Homework!" groaned Archie, sticking out his tongue in the mirror to prove that he was still as childish as ever. "Yuk!"

"Archie!" Mum's voice bellowed from the kitchen. "Your breakfast's ready."

Archie bounded downstairs, four steps at a time, surfed on the rug across the polished hall floor and launched himself like a rocket into a chair by the kitchen table.

"Archie a big boy!" shouted his little sister Molly, looking at him adoringly over her cereal bowl. "Archie do homework now!"

"Oh don't you start!" Archie snapped.

"You look great, love," said Mum, smiling sympathetically. "But you'd look even better with a smile!"

Archie didn't intend to smile. He'd never liked going to school, especially after the long summer holiday, and this year it was even worse! The year four teacher had apparently been taken ill during the summer so he had no idea whose class he would be in. Archie's friend from up the road, Barmy Ben, as he was nicknamed, had found out from somewhere that the replacement teacher was called Miss Bigbum. Archie thought that was probably highly unlikely, but he couldn't get the image of a doddery old lady with an extremely huge bottom out of his mind!

He gobbled down his cornflakes and sneakily drank the milk from his bowl when no one was looking.

"Come on, grab your bags, love," said Mum, picking up the car keys. "We'd better not be late on your first day back."

Archie stood up slowly.

"Come on Molly, hurry up and climb in the car," Mum continued, heading out of the door.

Molly, who much to Archie's annoyance, always seemed to

do just what Mum said, jumped down
from the chair immediately, not noticing a
glass of orange juice balanced precariously
near the edge of the table.

"Look out, Molly!" Archie screeched.

It was too late! Archie watched
helplessly as the glass flew into the air
sending orange juice pouring into his lap.

He sprang up, a huge wet patch
spreading from the top of his trousers all the way down one leg.

"Mum!" he screamed at the top of his voice. "Look what
Molly's done!"

Mum quickly ran back inside.

"Calm down, Archie," she scolded. "Molly wouldn't do it
on purpose. Just go upstairs and put on your trousers from last
year."

"But they're too small," groaned Archie.

"Just put them on or we'll be late!" Mum snapped, rapidly
losing patience.

Standing back in front of his bedroom mirror Archie stared
woefully at his old trousers dangling halfway between his feet
and his knees. He must have grown more than he thought in
the holidays; he couldn't wear those, everyone would laugh at
him! Then he had an idea. Quickly he swapped back into the
rather uncomfortable, soggy trousers, whilst at the same time
trying madly to remember his Sunday school lesson from the
previous day. Johnny, his teacher, had oozed enthusiasm as he

retold the story of God rescuing the people of Israel from the Egyptians.

"As Pharaoh and all his army approached," he had announced in a booming voice, "Moses held out his staff over the water and God blew with his wind and the sea dried up! The Israelites crossed through the Red Sea on dry ground ... God had saved them!"

He had nodded vigorously, eyeballing each child in turn, "You see, children, God can do anything!"

Archie glanced down again.

"Surely," he muttered, "if God can dry up the Red Sea my trousers will be no problem!"

He shut his eyes.

"Lord ..."

He paused and put his hands together hoping that it would have more effect.

"Lord, please dry my trousers!" he bellowed, trying to sound as much like Johnny as possible.

He half-opened one eye and peered down, sighing in disappointment.

"Maybe I'm not quite as important as the Israelites," he mumbled sadly, another idea forming in his head.

He whizzed off his jumper and began to tie it at different angles round his waist, viewing himself carefully to see which position made him look least like he hadn't made it to the toilet.

Once satisfied, he bounded back downstairs, threw his coat around himself and ran out to the car before his mum could spot his trick.

The journey to school was subdued for three reasons. First, Mum had noticed, (as mums always do,) the trouser/jumper trick, and Archie was therefore in trouble. Secondly, Archie was having all kinds of strange images flashing through his head of his new teacher and her huge bottom, and he was actually very frightened! Thirdly, he was madly trying to plan in detail how to avoid Mrs Dimple, the headteacher, whose main hate in life was jumpers tied around children's waists!

## Chapter 2

# THE NEW TEACHER

At the school gates Archie waved goodbye to Mum and Molly and ran round the side of the school with Barmy Ben and Patsy Primrose. Patsy was Archie's most unlikely friend. Her family was known to be the richest in the school, and probably in the town! Her brown hair was always tied in neat bunches and she never seemed to have even one crumple in her clothes. She had a huge swimming pool in her garden, was by far the cleverest in the class and her parents had tried everything possible to stop her from being friends with Archie! Nothing had worked and they had eventually given up in the hope that she would grow out of wanting to be friends with a boy.

Archie told them about his trouser problem.

"Oh, poor you," said Patsy sympathetically. "I suppose God's a bit busy saving the planet at the moment, with global warming and all that. Anyway we'll try and help you avoid Mrs Dimple if we can! I'll try to get her talking while you sneak inside."

"I dreamt about Miss Bigbum last night!" Ben announced dramatically as they settled down on a bench to wait for the bell. "She shouted at me so loudly that my 'ead exploded and then when you got your work wrong Archie, she sat on you!"

Patsy giggled but Archie winced. "Was I completely flattened?" he asked seriously.

"Completely!" replied Ben, equally soberly.

"She's probably quite nice really," said Patsy.

"It's OK for you, good little Patsy," complained Archie. "They all like you. They think you're little Miss Perfect!"

"If only they knew the truth," laughed Ben, punching Patsy teasingly.

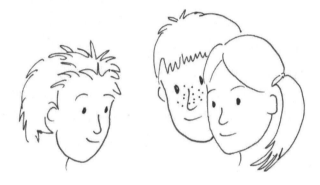

The bell rang loudly and they moved into line.

"Well done Patsy Primrose, the first in line again!" Mrs Dimple smiled a sickly sweet smile and patted Patsy on the head. She peered round; the look on her face suggesting her next comment would not be quite so cheerful.

"Archibald Edwards! Are you and Ben allowed to stand together? I am sure I banned you last term!"

Archie groaned inwardly, he hadn't done anything yet except stand in a line and already he'd been told off in front of the whole school.

"Now the hard bit," he thought to himself, glancing down. "I need to somehow get past Dimple features, get my coat off and get into the classroom so I can sit down and no one can see my trousers."

He heard Patsy's voice.

"Mrs Dimple, I do hope you had a lovely holiday. Did you go anywhere nice?"

"Good old Patsy," thought Archie as he saw her move round slightly as she talked so that Mrs Dimple was facing away from the door. He grabbed his opportunity, and running at the speed of light, zoomed to the front of the line and disappeared into the cloakroom.

He hung up his coat at top speed and dived into the classroom. The door was just closing behind him as Mrs D's booming voice echoed along the corridor.

"Archibald, is that jumper on properly?"

He was slightly taken aback to see a young, pretty, dark-haired woman standing in the corner of the classroom. For a moment he wondered if God had sent an angel to deliver some dry trousers! He looked at her closely.

"No, definitely not," he decided feeling slightly disappointed. "No halo and no wings!"

He glanced round for Miss Bigbum.

"Maybe she's ill," he thought suddenly, enjoying a delightful rush of excitement.

He had just decided that the lady was the mother of a new child who must be starting in the class, when she spoke to him.

"So you're Archibald are you?"

Archie nodded rather puzzled.

"Nice to meet you, Archibald. I'm Miss Bingham, your new teacher."

For a brief moment Archie found himself totally unable to move. His lower jaw dropped open as he feebly begun to mutter, "B ... b ... but you've got a small bott—"

He stopped himself just in time, and squeaked "Hello".

"Now, Archibald, Mrs Dimple wants you to put your jumper on. Is there a problem with that?"

Archie looked straight into her eyes and knew he had no choice but to tell the truth. Glancing round he muttered, "Me sister spilt her drink," as he gave Miss Bingham a flash of his wet trousers!

"Oh dear!"

Miss Bingham was smiling and her face lit up with a warm glow, her twinkling eyes filling Archie with relief.

"Well, you'd better put on your jumper like Mrs Dimple says, but I have a spare one here that you can tie round you, and if we move your place onto this table near the radiator," she swapped over two name cards. "You should dry out pretty quickly!"

Archie uttered an amazed "Thank you Miss" and sat down.

The rest of the class sauntered in and found their places. Everyone was silent, most mouths open. Sitting opposite Archie, Ben mouthed, "Look at the size of her bottom, it can't be her!" He was interrupted.

"Good morning everyone. My name is Miss Bingham." Her voice was lovely and gentle. "You came in beautifully and quietly. I hope you do that all the time! I hope as well that all of you are as polite as Archibald was this morning."

Everyone looked round wondering if there was a new boy. Archibald looked round too, surely she couldn't mean him!

Miss Bingham paused, "Don't you get called Archibald, then?" she asked Archie, appearing surprised by everybody's reaction.

"No Miss, I get Archie," mumbled Archie still wondering if she had honestly called him polite!

"Well, Archie it is then," said Miss Bingham. "Now let's take the register."

## Chapter 3

# A WINK AND A WHISPER

"Yes, Miss Bingham, Miss Bingham, Miss Bingham," Archie practiced quietly as he waited for his name to be called for registration.

"Whatever I do I mustn't say the 'big bum' bit," he thought to himself. "Not when she thinks I'm polite!"

"Archie Edwards!" the voice called.

"Yes, Miss Bingham."

Archie's voice was so loud and clear and precise that half the class began to giggle!

"Thank you, that was lovely and clear, Archie." Miss Bingham smiled and continued down the list of names.

She shut the register and glanced round. "Ben, will you take the register to the office for me?" she asked. "You can pick someone to go with you."

Ben jumped up. "I'll take Archie, Miss."

For a moment Archie groaned inwardly. The last thing he wanted to do was to leave the classroom in soggy trousers with Mrs Dimple waiting to pounce at any moment.

A sudden movement to his left made him sigh with relief. Henrietta's hand had shot up like a bullet from a gun! She was the class telltale. Her full name was Henrietta McTellier but everyone called her Henrietta McTell-Tale. Usually she drove

Archie mad, but today it seemed as if she was going to be his saviour!

As she spoke her voice rang with triumph and her smug face glowed with pleasure.

"Ben and Archie aren't allowed out of the classroom together, Miss. When they were in reception class Mrs Dimple said they would never, ever be allowed out on their own again!"

Ben glowered at her, but Archie felt quite relieved.

"Is that true Ben?" Miss Bingham looked confused.

"Y ... y ... y ... yes, M ... m ... m ... Miss."

Ben always stammered when he was embarrassed.

"Why on earth is that?"

"W ... w ... w ... well, M ... m ... Miss, A ... A ... Archie'll explain ..."

Archie stuck his tongue out at Henrietta and began to speak.

"Well, Miss, it's like this. When me and Ben were in reception class we were allowed to take the register to the office three times ..."

He paused.

"The first time we had only been in school for five days and we decided to escape and run away. Mrs Dimple looked for us for three hours and eventually found us in the park."

There was a murmur of giggling round the room.

Archie took a deep breath and continued.

"The second time we got lost and ended up in the kitchen ... we ate all the biscuits that Cook had made for dinner ... and then Ben was sick in the hall!"

More giggling.

Archie braced himself. "The third time we decided to look in the PE cupboard on the way back but we heard someone coming and shut the door ... we couldn't open it again and we didn't dare shout. We never got found until after dinner. I was asleep in the beanbag box and Ben was snoring in the football kit! Mrs Dimple had called the police!"

By now most of the class were laughing uncontrollably.

"So," Henrietta butted in with glee, "Mrs Dimple said they can never go anywhere on their own again."

Miss Bingham looked very much like she would like to laugh. She was quiet for a moment and then swallowed a few times before she spoke.

"Well it seems to me that no one should be punished for something they did almost three years ago. I believe everyone can change and everybody deserves a second chance. However, I'd better speak to Mrs Dimple before I make any decision, so Rachel you go with Ben today."

She turned and bent her head towards Archie's ear.

"Gets you out of being seen with your two jumpers on," she whispered, winking at him.

Archie found himself grinning from ear to ear. He'd never had a teacher whisper to him before. Usually they shouted at him, or roared at him if it were Mrs Dimple! But here was this new, pretty, small-bottomed teacher who actually seemed to like him.

"Wow," thought Archie, "maybe this year won't be too bad after all."

Ben and Rachel returned shortly and sat down. Archie gave Ben the thumbs up sign, raising his eye brows and smirking knowingly.

Ben blushed and frowned at him ferociously. In the reception class Ben had announced to Archie that when he grew up he was going to marry Rachel Brown. That was three years ago and Archie had never let him forget it! The truth was that Ben still did like Rachel and had been secretly delighted to take the register with her. He would, however, never admit to it, not even to his best friend; in fact especially not to his best friend!

The time up until break was spent talking. Miss Bingham

seemed to want to know all about the children. She asked them about their brothers and sisters, their pets, their favourite food and what they liked doing. Archie was amazed at some of the things that were said and listened intently. He never would have imagined that quiet little Chandi would have a pet snake or that Joshua lived with foster parents. He was stunned when George said that his dad had been in a wheelchair since a motorbike accident two years ago; and when Lucy said that she had eight brothers and sisters and no mum and that her dad couldn't get a job, he suddenly understood why sometimes she was dressed rather differently to everyone else.

Then it was Miss Bingham's turn, and the class listened in fascination. No teacher had ever told them anything about themselves before, which had led to all sorts of stories being made up!

Rumour had it that Mrs Dimple was so large because she had had 47 children of her own so that she could practice being a headteacher at home. Apparently she called the register at breakfast every morning, after which the family had to line up quietly and march past her to have their uniform checked.

Rumour also had it that Mr Scott, the deputy head, had once been arrested for being a pirate and smuggling toilet paper into the country. The basis for that rumour seemed to be the way he shouted, "Aa-haargh!" every time he found somebody hiding in the boy's loo!

Miss Bingham seemed quite normal. She had been teaching for two years in a different school. She lived on her own in a small house, she played netball, went to church, liked going out with her friends, liked cooking and, to Archie's relief, liked children! Archie and his friends had often discussed why so many people became teachers when they really seemed to dislike children very much indeed!

The bell for playtime sounded. Archie glanced up at the clock. One and a half hours gone and he hadn't had to write a word!

"Wow," he mumbled to himself. "I think I can live with this!"

## Chapter 4

# CATERPILLARS ARE BEST!

The start of the year assembly was usually boring. It always lasted a full hour with Mrs Dimple droning on and on about fresh starts and how each child had a chance to begin again, with all the old behaviour from last year cancelled out and a new chapter beginning. This year was exactly the same. Archie had a desperate urge to put up his hand and ask why, if new starts were available, he had been told off the minute he stepped into line. He resisted the urge and concentrated on not falling asleep!

After twenty minutes of explaining what she meant by good behaviour, Mrs Dimple moved on to her story.

"Today, children," she began. "I am going to tell you a beautiful story about metamorphosis. Can anyone tell me what metamorphosis is?"

Most of the children looked completely blank, having switched off from listening within the first thirty seconds of arriving in the hall. Only Sui Chang's hand shot up.

"Yes, Sui."

"Is it when a caterpillar changes into a butterfly Miss?"

"Well done!" Mrs Dimple gave him one of the looks that she saved for only the cleverest of children.

Archie looked at Sui in admiration. He was in year six, two years older than Archie. How he wished that one day he,

Archibald Edwards, could be clever like that. He shut his eyes and began to imagine.

He was in the hall. Mrs Dimple was asking the children the hardest question she had ever asked. She was convinced that no one of their age could possibly know the answer, but

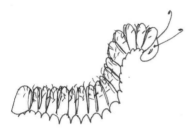

Archie did! He put up his hand and answered correctly. All the younger children were looking at him, whispering quietly, "I wish I was like him."

His dreams were interrupted as Mrs Dimple reached the great crescendo of her story.

"So, all of you, even if you've been a caterpillar in the past, could become a beautiful butterfly. You could change from an ugly caterpillar into something we would be proud to have in our school!"

Archie quite wished he'd listened to the first part of the story so that he might have understood the ending. He felt rather sorry for a caterpillar being called ugly, especially when

he actually preferred caterpillars to butterflies. Caterpillars were fascinating to watch. In fact he liked nothing better than his mum finding a caterpillar in the cauliflower when she was making tea. He could watch them for hours moving slowly and methodically on their miniature legs, nibbling tiny holes in the leaves. Butterflies he thought were rather boring. He agreed that they were pretty, but they always flitted around quickly and were never still long enough for you to get a proper look at them.

"Archibald Edwards, I asked you a question!"

Archie came back into the real world to find that now hundreds of eyes actually were staring at him.

"Archibald Edwards, I said 'what would you rather be?'"

"A caterpillar, Miss!" Archie knew the answer was wrong as soon as he said it.

"Archibald Edwards, I despair of you! We are going to pray now, and I suggest that you pray harder than anyone!"

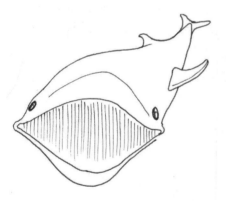

The prayer was a very long one. Mrs Dimple asked God to help all the children, especially naughty little boys who wanted to be caterpillars, to be good all through the year. Archie prayed that God would send a big fish, like in the story of Jonah, who would swallow him up so he could escape from Mrs Dimple!

Everyone said "Amen," and lifted their heads.

Archie kept his head bowed for a moment longer urgently telling God that, just in case He was going to answer, he would rather the big fish swallowed Mrs Dimple instead of him as he wanted to play with his friends at break time!

When Archie did lift his head he glanced round expectantly, but he couldn't spot a big fish. He did however catch Miss Bingham looking at him sympathetically. She gave him the kind of look that, although he had never seen before, Archie somehow understood.

"She likes caterpillars too," he thought to himself, and he smiled.

"Now children, just before you leave the hall, I have a special treat for you." Mrs Dimple grinned from child to child as if something wonderful was about to happen.

"During the holidays I have written a song for you all. It is a song about our school and it is to the tune of 'Twinkle, Twinkle Little Star'."

She nodded to Mrs Grimshaw at the piano who began with the usual incorrect note. Mrs Dimple's out of tune voice sang out in pride.

"Little children good and sweet,
Should be tidy, should be neat.
Should be good in all they do,
Not like animals in a zoo.
Little children all this term
Be quiet, perfect, quick to learn."

Archie felt Jamil, who was sitting next to him, poke him sharply in the ribs. He looked up to see Jamil stick two fingers in his mouth pretending to be sick. They both began to giggle and then stopped suddenly when they realised that Miss Bingham was watching them. She frowned and put her finger to her lips, but Archie felt sure there was a definite look of amusement in her eyes.

Dinnertime was as uneventful as it usually was when the weather was nice enough for the children to play on the field. Archie, Ben and Jamil played football most of the time, stopping only once to watch the girls doing handstands.

Sitting back at his desk, Archie found himself almost looking forward to the afternoon.

"Now everyone," Miss Bingham began. "As we didn't manage to do any literacy this morning, we are going to spend the afternoon writing poetry!"

All Archie's good feelings rolled away and before he realised it he let out an agonised groan.

Miss Bingham jumped. "What's the matter Archie, are you ill?"

"No, Miss … sorry, Miss … I'm just rubbish at poems, Miss," he stuttered.

"Well Archie, just try your best, you may find you enjoy it."

"Not likely!" muttered Archie, just loud enough for his table to hear.

"Now," she continued, ignoring him. "This morning Mrs Dimple taught us all a new song and, by the looks on some of your faces, I think some of you thought you could do better!" She glanced sideways at Jamil who blushed as he remembered her seeing his sick sign.

"So firstly this afternoon we are going to have a go at

improving Mrs Dimple's verse and then we'll have a go at writing some of our own."

She uncovered a large flip chart with alternate lines of the song missing.

"Little children good and sweet,

\----------------------------------------

Should be good in all they do,

\----------------------------------------

Little children all this term

\----------------------------------------."

"Now I want you to let your imaginations flow. I'm going to say a line and I want you to say the first thing that comes into your heads. Ready?"

"'Little children good and sweet ...' Ben, you go first."

Ben gulped.

"I ... I ... I ... don't know."

"Just say anything, Ben." Miss Bingham was oozing enthusiasm.

"Anything that rhymes ... 'Little children good and sweet ...'"

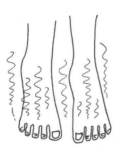

Ben swallowed hard and opened his mouth. "Should never have such stinky feet."

The words blurted out quickly and the class roared with laughter.

Ben looked in horror at Miss Bingham.

"I'm in trouble now," he thought.

But he was wrong. Miss Bingham was beaming.

"Brilliant, Ben!" she smiled. "Poems are meant to be fun. Let's make up silly ones and we can do the serious ones later. Archie you're next ... 'Little children good and sweet, Should never have such stinky feet. Should be good in all they do ...' Go on, Archie, say the next line."

Archie desperately wanted to impress, but as he opened his mouth he felt he was rapidly heading for disaster.

"Should be good in all they do, Should wee and poo upon the loo."

His voice trailed off as the class exploded.

"I ... er ... I couldn't think of nothin' else, Miss," he muttered guiltily.

"Archie, it's fine," said Miss Bingham, laughing. "I don't think we'll be singing this one in assembly, but what you said rhymes and that's what I asked for."

For the rest of the lesson the children were split into twos and could make up as many silly versions of the song as they wanted, as long as they had one sensible verse before the time limit ran out. Archie was partnered with Jack, a quiet boy who was good at football but average at lessons. Neither of them fancied their chances at poetry.

Most of the lesson seemed to be spent in hysterical laughter. Miss Bingham wandered round encouraging everyone and reading some of the verses. Ten minutes from the end she reminded everyone that they needed to have produced one sensible version and, to Archie and Jack's amazement, they found that their brains seemed to be in gear for rhyming things and they were actually happy with the result.

"In our school we should be glad,

Help people when they are sad.

Care for others, do our work.

Always try hard, never shirk.

Make the world a better place,

Keep a smile upon our face."

Miss Bingham read it out and there was a stunned silence. Jack nudged Archie.

"Did we really write that?" he whispered.

Archie shrugged, "I suppose we must have!" he whispered back. "Or else it's a miracle!"

"Well done you two! That is brilliant, and Archie, I thought you said you couldn't do poetry!"

Miss Bingham's eyes twinkled at him.

"But … but … I couldn't do it, Miss!" Archie looked confused.

"Well, Archie, it seems that you can do it now. Well done."

Patsy caught his eye and grinned at him across the room.

"Swot!" she mouthed.

Archie stuck out his tongue at her, raised his eyebrows and gave a silly grin. He rather liked the idea of being a swot!

# Chapter 5

# MODEL PLANE

**A**rchie amazed his mum at the end of the first day. As normal, he came out of school smiling, ready to escape into the real world and play football in the garden. It was the answer to her usual question, "Have you had a good day, love?" that was unexpected.

Normally Archie would pull a face and say, "No!" in a sullen, rather rude manner. Today he replied, "Yeah, brilliant!" with such enthusiasm that his Mum couldn't think of anything else to say and they walked to the car in silence.

Archie said little about school when he arrived home, apart from announcing gleefully that he had no homework. He played with Molly in the garden, watched TV and sat down for tea just as Dad arrived home from the fire station. Archie was very proud of his dad. Most of the kids in his class thought it was great to have a dad who was a firefighter and Archie knew they would have been well impressed today when he appeared in the doorway with black soot still on his face and neck.

"Pooey, Daddy, you smell!" shouted Molly quickly deciding not to give him a kiss or cuddle.

"I know, sorry love," said Dad. "I'll just whizz upstairs and have a shower then I'll tell you about my day."

Archie always loved to hear about Dad's adventures. His favourite story was one that had happened in the middle of the night. The firefighters were called to a huge house with an indoor swimming pool at the back of it. It was a large, impressive fire, and once it was under control one of the chief officers in the county turned up to check what was going on. The electricity had obviously been turned off to avoid danger, so the only lights were those on the fire engine. The

chief officer had marched in with his head held high, ready to take command, and had immediately fallen straight into the swimming pool with a huge splash!

Today nothing so amusing had happened but Archie's day was quite forgotten as they chatted about other things. It was only later when he climbed into bed and his Mum came to say goodnight, that school was mentioned at all.

"So, love," said Mum, determined to find something out. "You had a good day? You liked your teacher then?"

"Mum." Archie looked quite shy. "She's really nice and … I think she likes me. She said I'm polite and write good poems!"

Mum smiled at him and stroked his hair.

"I'm sure she likes you Archie. She would be silly not to."

"I bet she won't like me much when I get into trouble!"

muttered Archie. "I don't think I can be good forever, even if I try my hardest!"

Mum smiled again. "Always try your best to be good, Archie. But never forget that God made you just the way you are. He's proud of what He made and He loves you very much!"

She stood up and kissed his head.

"Dad and I love you very much too," she said quietly. "And it's lovely to see you so happy."

She pulled his bedroom door shut and flicked on the landing light. Archie rolled his eyes. He liked to be in complete darkness to get to sleep but, ever since Molly had dreamt that aliens from outer space had invaded their house and stolen the goldfish, they had had to keep a light on to stop the aliens from returning to pinch the cat! Why Mum and Dad hadn't just told her the truth and explained that actually it was Tabby, the cat, who had eaten the goldfish in the middle of the night he couldn't understand!

A shaft of light fell onto a model aeroplane that Archie had made during the summer holidays. He climbed out of bed and wandered across his room, carefully avoiding the creaky floorboards. Mum always got cross if they got out of bed unless they were about to be sick!

Gently he ran his finger over the model Spitfire. It had taken him three whole weeks to finish it! He had needed a tiny bit of help but nearly the whole thing was his own work. He knew

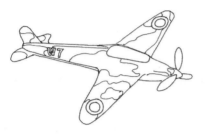

it wasn't absolutely perfect; his hand had wobbled as he was painting the name on the side and there was a huge smear across the underside where his hand had slipped with the glue. But the little faults didn't matter, in fact he thought those made it even better; it meant there wasn't another model like it anywhere in the world!

He snuggled back into bed.

"God made you, Archie, and He's proud of what He made." His mum's words kept playing through his mind.

"Could it be," he thought, "could it really be that God is proud of me like I'm proud of my Spitfire? I know my model's not perfect but to me it's the best in the world! God knows all my little faults ..." He paused and pulled a guilty face, quickly correcting himself. "Er, big faults, but he's still proud of me because he made me! ... Wow!!"

Archie had a dream that night. The aliens returned for the cat! Tabby put up a good fight but was eventually cornered in Archie's bedroom. Suddenly the engines on the Spitfire began to roar; Tabby leapt into the cockpit and zoomed out of the open window!

The aliens looked down at Archie sleeping peacefully.

"It is the boy," they said in robotic voices. "It is the boy that God made. We will take him with us and make others like him."

With that they picked Archie up and marched him back to the waiting ship!

There was nothing the sleeping boy could do to stop them until, with a loud "Meeeooooww!" Tabby returned, soaring through the air! With one swoosh of his paw he grasped Archie, dragging him into the copilot's seat. Together they flew the plane to a far-off ocean, the aliens in hot pursuit! Suddenly they dived down, down towards the water and, as they swooped back up, a huge fish lurched out of the sea and swallowed the alien's spaceship in his enormous mouth!

Archie woke up, sweat pouring off him, extremely relieved to be safely in his own bed, Tabby curled up next to him purring loudly!

He planted a magnificent kiss on the startled cat!

"I will never kick you again, my hero!" he announced. "And I will buy Molly a new goldfish with my pocket money, just so that you can have a bit of fun!"

## Chapter 6

# GOOD AT MATHS!

The rest of the week passed in a blur for Archie. He had managed a full week of not being sent to Mrs Dimple's office, he had not been kept in at playtime, he had finished quite a lot of his work and he had actually not dreaded going to school on any day. Miss Bingham had been declared the nicest teacher in the school by nearly everyone in the class. Henrietta McTell-Tale still wasn't keen. Miss Bingham had said that she didn't want any tales being told about mistakes children had made in the past and so Henrietta had been silent for a whole week. After discussion with Mrs Dimple, Archie and Ben were made the permanent register monitors and had taken a trip to the office every day without any mishap.

On Friday afternoon the whole school found themselves sitting once again in assembly, half an hour before home time. Archie usually dreaded this part of the week. Mrs Dimple always used this as an opportunity to point out which children had misbehaved and needed to try harder in future. Archie's name always came up, although as he thought about it he didn't see how he could be mentioned today as he hadn't been in trouble even once!

His thoughts were interrupted by Mrs Dimple's high-pitched squeak. "Archibald Edwards come out here, and Jack Jones too."

Archie stood up feeling cross.

"It's not fair," he thought. "I'm sure I haven't done anything wrong."

He stopped next to Mrs Dimple, noticing Jack's bright red face. He could see Ben and Patsy looking genuinely sorry for him and Henrietta looking completely full of glee!

"Now boys and girls," Mrs Dimple continued. "We have two very clever children in this school. Miss Bingham has passed on to me a verse of a song that Archibald and Jack wrote earlier this week. You may remember that I had written a school song, well, they have copied my idea, and I have to say it is very good."

Archie bent sideways and whispered in Jack's ear. "I hope she hasn't got the rude one." Jack pulled a face and blushed again at the thought of it!

Suddenly Archie and Jack's verse appeared on the screen and Mrs Dimple read through it.

"Now, school," she declared. "We are all going to sing it together. Are we ready?"

She nodded to Mrs Grimshaw and the music began.

"In our school we should be glad,

Help people when they are sad.

Care for others, do our work.

Always try hard, never shirk.

Make the world a better place,

Keep a smile upon our face."

Archie wasn't sure what he felt standing at the front while everyone sang his words. A bit of him felt rather proud, and in his mind he could see his mum's face glowing with pride when he told her (if he told her) later! Another part of him felt very different. He could see the faces of his classmates. Ben seemed to be unable to control his shoulders going up and down; he was very red in the face and had tears in his eyes; Jamil was sticking just one finger in and out of his mouth whenever he thought the teachers weren't looking! Others looked impressed; some almost slightly jealous, some of them looked totally amused and some totally uninterested!

Once the song was over Mrs Dimple sent the boys back to their seats. Archie couldn't stop himself taking a little bow to the audience. That set Ben off giggling much more and, because he was trying to hold it in, resulted in a most enormous hiccup, which made the whole school laugh.

"Archibald Edwards, will you never learn?!" moaned Mrs Dimple angrily as she fought to regain control.

Archie sat down sheepishly, relieved that he could still make everyone laugh and hadn't turned into a complete angel!

It was award time. Every Friday each teacher was allowed to give two gold star badges to members of the class. The awards could be for anything. Children got them for being kind or helpful, for excellent work or any other notable things. The stars were accompanied by a certificate stating why they had been awarded. Archie clearly remembered why he had been given them in the past.

'Awarded for …

… not shouting out as much as normal.

… only being sent to Mrs Dimple four times in one week.

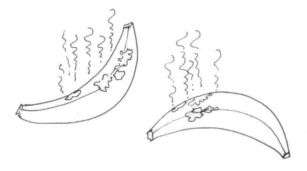

… removing a mouldy banana from his very messy drawer.'

In fact, every award that Archie had ever been given had a ring of criticism to it. He pretended that he didn't mind, but deep down it made him quite sad.

"Patsy Primrose, you have an award from Miss Bingham for excellent work in literacy. Well done!"

Patsy sprang up and moved quickly to the front. Archie was pleased. Patsy was always well behaved, always got on with her work and hardly ever got the gold star as teachers seemed to think that she didn't need any encouragement. He smiled his approval to Miss Bingham and gave her the thumbs up sign. She smiled back.

"Archibald Edwards, come out here!"

Archie gulped, giving the thumbs up sign to a teacher, now he was for it. He walked out slowly.

"Archibald, Miss Bingham is giving you the gold star this week for excellent maths."

Archie stood rooted to the spot.

"Excellent maths!"

The words rang in his ears. He looked round at Miss Bingham who smiled and gave him the thumbs up sign this time.

Archie never knew what happened next. Children from the other year groups came out to join the line of winners, but Archie didn't notice. He gazed out at the sea of faces, his head held high and his chest out. He, Archibald Edwards, was excellent at maths! It was the greatest moment of his life!

*   *   *

It was home time and it was pouring with rain. Every child in the class had their coats tightly fastened round them as they collected their bags to go home; everyone that is apart from Archie. Miss Bingham noticed and said nothing; she knew he wanted to show off his award.

She watched as he ran up to his mum and heard his voice above all the hubbub of the crowds.

"I am excellent at maths."

She saw his Mum grinning and turned away to go and tidy up the classroom.

"Bye, Miss Bingham."

She turned back and waved at the soaking wet, dripping but happy boy.

"Well," she said to herself. "Those trousers are wetter than when he arrived on Monday morning, but his face is like the face of a different boy!"

## Chapter 7

# THE ESCAPE PLAN

The first two and a half weeks of term passed quickly. Archie had certainly not been perfect, but he had somehow avoided serious trouble. Miss Bingham had told him off for burping repeatedly during lunch, for making loud tractor noises when concentrating, for putting his finger over the end of the tap soaking everyone nearby, and for writing a pretend love letter to Henrietta from Jamil. However, she hadn't seemed overly concerned and somehow the way she told him off made Archie feel like he wanted to try harder, rather than making him feel like the most horrible boy on the planet.

Now however, as Archie lay in bed, he felt thoroughly miserable. It was Wednesday night and for the next two days Miss Bingham was going on a course to learn how to teach science better. Archie couldn't understand why she had to go. She had already taught him for three science lessons and he was sure that she knew everything there was to know about the subject. Miss Bingham had warned the class the day before that she would be absent and that Mrs Dimple would be taking them instead. She had looked directly at Archie and raised her eyebrows when she said 'Mrs Dimple', as if she had known what he would be thinking. Archie hoped desperately that she couldn't really read his mind, as his thoughts had not been very polite at all!

He suddenly remembered the memory verse he'd learnt in Sunday school.

"The Lord knows all the thoughts of man."

"I suppose that means boys as well," he mumbled under his breath, wondering if it were possible that God had been asleep and had missed what he had been thinking. Immediately another verse sprang into his mind.

"He who watches over you will not sleep!"

Archie rolled his eyes. "Seems I can escape from teachers but not God," he muttered, as a plan of escape from Mrs Dimple began to form in his head.

He had pretended to feel ill from the moment he got home from school. At teatime he even announced that he wasn't hungry so his act would be more convincing. At first his mum believed him and tucked him up, under a duvet, on the settee. He had soon discovered, however, that he was absolutely starving and, despite his greatest efforts not to be seen, Mum had eventually found him under the stairs with chocolate all round his mouth and fourteen chocolate biscuit wrappers in his pocket. He knew then that the game was up!

Archie had been severely told off, banned from biscuits for a week and sent to bed. He had lain awake for a while, his stomach rumbling loudly, before slowly drifting off to sleep.

It was 4.30 a.m. when he woke suddenly, a new escape plan whirling in his mind. He had seen it in a film. It hadn't worked then, but he felt sure that he could manage it. Quietly he tiptoed into Mum and Dad's room and picked up Mum's lipstick. Then without a sound he crept into the bathroom, silently removed his pyjama top and carefully drew spots all over his chest and face. Archie wasn't certain what size chickenpox spots were meant to be so he drew a variety of

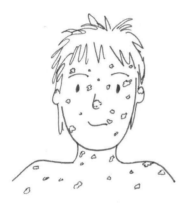 different shapes and sizes and then rolled up his pyjama bottoms and finished the job.

Returning carefully to bed he lay still for a moment deciding what to do next. Then in his most pathetic, desperate, croaking voice he called, "Mummy, oh Mummy, come quickly. I think I'm ill!"

No one appeared so he tried it again a bit louder. This time he heard the bed creak, but no footsteps sounded.

He tried again, only this time he added loudly, "Does no one care about me? I'm going to chuck!"

Both Mum and Dad scampered into his room and flicked on the light.

"Oh Archie," said Mum, looking very concerned for about two seconds.

Her voice changed. "Why are you covered in lipstick dots?"

"I'm not, they're chickenpox," said Archie suddenly feeling very silly.

"Oh no, they're not." Dad was annoyed. "Go back to sleep and we'll clean you up in the morning. We are not amused!"

He flicked off the light sharply and marched out.

Archie lay still for the next three hours, dozing in and out of sleep, not wanting to move in case he smudged lipstick all over the pillow and got into even worse trouble. Gradually the room grew lighter and the birds began their dawn chorus.

"What am I going to do?" he thought to himself, wishing he hadn't been so daft. Looking down at his spotty legs he decided that at least Mum and Dad would be happier if he were clean. He crept into the bathroom, ran a shallow bath and began to scrub … he added more warm water … he added bubble bath and scrubbed again …

and again … and again. A queer feeling of horror began to fill him. The bright shiny appearance of the spots had definitely lessened, but the left over ingrained pinkish marks refused to budge!

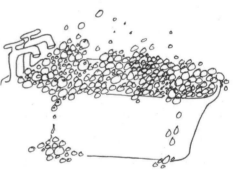

By the time his bleary-eyed mum appeared Archie was close to tears.

"It won't come off," he cried out in panic. "I'm going to be pink for ever! Everyone will think I'm a Barbie!"

"Calm down, Archie," said his Mum trying not to laugh. "Maybe this will teach you a lesson. Let me have a go."

It was no use. Mum's amazing collection of wipes and creams made the marks appear less obvious, but they were definitely still there. Mum forced Archie into his school uniform and made him close his eyes while she had one last scrub.

"There, you don't look too bad," she said in the most unconvincing voice Archie had ever heard her use.

Slowly he opened his eyes and peeped in the mirror, bursting into a sudden exclamation.

"I can't go to school like this! I look like a gone-wrong clown!"

Archie pointed to the largest spot covering most of his nose.

"You have no choice, Archie," said his mum in a voice that Archie didn't dare disobey. "You shouldn't have done it in the first place."

Archie arrived at school in a major strop. His Mum had found something called foundation that covered most of the 'chickenpox,' but his nose was so deeply ingrained that it made little difference to that part of his face. Archie remembered how he had rubbed the lipstick round and round on his nose, hoping to get the most dramatic effect. He cringed. It was going to have a dramatic effect alright, but not the one he had hoped for.

Jamil saw him first.

"Accident with the makeup Archie?" he sniggered.

"Just don't ask," mumbled Archie. "Just come and play football with me quickly."

They sped off.

"Archibald Edwards, what have you done to your face?!"

Mrs Dimple's voice echoed along the line to the very back where Archie stood hiding behind Ben with his head down.

"How on earth can she see me face from there?" he mumbled.

"Bionic eyes," said Ben seriously.

"Archibald, come here!"

Archie headed towards the front, conscious of the ripple of laughter as he passed each child.

"What have you done?"

"I was being a clown, Miss." He didn't want to tell her the whole truth.

"Well you look ridiculous, and today's the school photographs."

Archie swallowed.

"Oh no," he thought. "My silly clown nose recorded in a frame on the wall forever."

He remembered the long line of pictures, lovingly framed by his Mum, showing all the stages in his life from the day he had been born. He hoped that one day his Mum would be able to see the funny side of this one!

As they hung up their coats and moved into the classroom Archie tried his best to smile and joke, as if he couldn't care less about his appearance. Deep down he wanted the ground to open up and eat him.

In class things went from bad to worse. During registration he quietly tried to explain to Ben what had happened to him. He was so engrossed in telling his story that when his name was called, without thinking, he replied, "Yes, Mrs Pimple Stinkle!" —a nickname that lots of the children used in secret!

"Archibald Edwards come out here immediately!" ordered Mrs Dimple furiously.

Archie stood up and hurried to the front, not noticing Lucy's bag on the floor. He tripped over it, put his hands out to steady himself, collided with the flip chart and watched in horror as it slowly slid over, landing with a bang on Mrs Dimple's head!

"Archibald!" she roared, going red in the face.

For a moment Archie thought she might actually thump him. Instead he spent the next hour outside her office which, although boring, at least meant he wasn't with her. By the end of the morning Archie calculated that he had been told off 38 times. Jamil commented that it must be some kind of record, as he had only spent one hour and three minutes in the classroom, and Ben challenged him to try to make it 60 'tellings off' by the end of the day!

At lunchtime Archie was positioned next to Patsy in the dining hall as usual. At the start of term he had overheard the dinner ladies saying that Patsy would be a good influence on him and might stop him firing peas at people or sticking pieces of carrot up his nose, pretending he had a cold! In truth it worked well. Patsy and he would have a laugh but they were usually fairly sensible. Today however, he saw no point in behaving.

"If Mrs Dimple thinks I'm bad, I might as well be horrible," he announced as he squashed a tomato on his nose and held a triangular piece of pizza on his head like a hat.

"Look at me!" he shouted. "I really am a clown!"

Everyone laughed. Everyone, that is, except for Mrs Dimple, who entered the hall just in time to see Archie juggling with three pieces of cucumber.

Her voice split the air.

"Archibald, get to my office!"

"39," whispered Archie as he passed Ben, who mouthed, "Only 21 to go!"

By home time Archie had exceeded all expectations. He had been rude, had three fights, been sent off in football practice, produced messy work and achieved a grand total of 64 tellings-off, which Jamil calculated as one every six minutes!

Mrs Dimple hovered ominously at the school gate waiting to pounce on Archie's unsuspecting Mum, and Archie felt dreadful.

"Mrs Edwards I need a word with you!" There was silence as every parent turned to stare. Mrs Edwards blushed. "Archibald has had a terrible day …"

Mrs Edwards looked at Archie with the look of disappointment that Archie dreaded. Then her look changed.

"Come here Archie," she said looking inquiringly at his face. She pulled him towards her and carefully lifted up his top. The skin on his chest and back was red and blotchy. Archie began to scratch vigorously.

"Archie, you're covered in a rash!" she exclaimed. "We need to get you to a doctor."

Mrs Dimple jumped back.

"Uurrgh, get him away. I don't want to catch it!" she screamed, immediately forgetting all the events of the day.

As Archie was marched to the car, he passed Jamil, who softly whispered, "You got out of that one nicely! Did you use paint this time?"

Archie shrugged and shook his head. He really didn't feel very well.

# Chapter 8

# JUST LIKE HIM!

Archie's visit to the doctor revealed that he was allergic to lipstick. The doctor gave him some revolting tasting medicine, some cream and special liquid to pour in the bath to stop the itching. To Archie's delight the doctor then announced that, as the rash may get worse before it got better, he would advise that Archie didn't go to school until it had gone, which may take a few days. Archie resisted the strong temptation to kiss him but couldn't stop himself shouting, "Whoopee! I've done it! I won't have the dreaded Pimple Stinkle tomorrow!" at the top of his voice.

Both Dr Jones and Mum laughed, although she told him off severely later!

On Sunday Mum pronounced him well enough to attend church, where the story of Jesus healing a man with spots all over his body seemed particularly apt!

"You see children," Johnny explained, "Jesus didn't run away from this man with the dreaded disease of leprosy, even though everybody knew that it was such an easy disease to catch. Instead he reached out his hand and touched him. He cared for everyone."

Archie remembered Mrs Dimple's face as she ran away from

him, shouting "Uurrgh" as soon as she had seen his rash. He wondered what Jesus would have done if he had been there when Mum lifted up his shirt. Archie felt sure that Jesus' reaction would have been very different.

By Monday morning Archie's rash was almost completely gone and the frequent soaks in the special bubble bath had removed all the chickenpox marks.

He was quite looking forward to seeing Miss Bingham again although he was certain that she would have been told all about Thursday's disaster and may be cross with him.

Ben was waiting for him at the gate.

"Is it true?" he asked eagerly. "Are you really allergic to lipstick?"

"Yep!" grinned Archie proudly. "So if I ever need another day off I just do my lips a few days before and hey presto I've done it!"

"Archie, you can't do that!" said Patsy running up and looking shocked.

Jamil butted in. "Does it mean that when you're older and want to kiss a girl you'll have to tell her to wash her face first?!" he questioned.

Archie looked horrified.

"Hey, I hadn't thought of that one," he said, blushing bright crimson. "Anyway, who wants to kiss girls—yuk!"

When Archie said good morning as he entered the classroom, he could tell that Miss Bingham knew all about Thursday. She smiled and said, "Good morning, Archie." But there was something in the tone of her voice that meant, 'I'm very disappointed with you.'

Archie felt miserable. He had told himself over and over during the weekend that he had been bad on Thursday because his body was coming out in a rash and he felt ill. However deep down he knew he'd been naughty because Mrs Dimple was taking the class and he didn't like her one bit.

At playtime Miss Bingham asked him to stay in for a chat. She sat on the desk next to him and looked down.

"Archie, I know all about Thursday," she said sadly. "Why did you have to be so naughty? I've been telling Mrs Dimple all term how you've changed and that you've worked so hard and been so sensible. Now she thinks I made it all up."

Archie looked up at her. Her eyes looked so kind and he knew that he had let her down badly.

"I'm sorry, I didn't mean to …" he spluttered. "But I wanted you, not her … she hates me and it's not fair!"

To his embarrassment he found that he was beginning to cry.

"Archie," continued Miss Bingham gently, "I know Mrs Dimple doesn't seem to understand you but you can't just decide to behave like that when I'm not there or it looks as if I'm not telling the truth about you."

"I'm sorry," sobbed Archie. He'd never felt so bad. This was the last person in the world he wanted to let down.

"I know you're sorry," said Miss Bingham firmly. "But you need to say sorry to Mrs Dimple."

"No way!"

"Listen Archie. I've explained to her that having an allergic reaction can make children do things that they wouldn't normally do …"

"But I would normally do them," Archie interrupted.

Miss Bingham ignored him and continued, "I think Mrs Dimple is willing to accept, this once, that you were ill … if you apologise."

Five minutes later Archie was pacing up and down the corridor outside Mrs Dimple's office praying that God would send an alien to take him to another planet.

Miss Bingham had sent him out to play but, in a moment of courage, he had cut through the yard and in at another door. He didn't want to do this but somehow he knew he must if Miss Bingham was to think well of him.

Knock knock!

Archie wanted to run away but his knees were shaking so much that there was no way he could do that!

"Come in!"

Archie pushed down the handle and walked in. There was

still no sign of an alien although Mrs Dimple did look even more like a ferocious dragon than he had noticed before.

"I'm sorry," he said as fast as he could. "I must have been ill!"

Mrs Dimple peered sternly over the top of her glasses.

"Archibald, Miss Bingham told me that you have been a different child this term. On Thursday you were a different child— you were even worse than normal! However, as you were about to be ill, I will forget about it, unless of course it happens again."

She glowered at him.

"Thank you, Miss," Archie muttered.

"Now go out to play …" she paused for a moment and to Archie's amazement she almost looked like she was going to smile! "It takes courage to say sorry— well done—and remember, you have a lot of making up to do."

Archie remembered to shut the door quietly behind him. Stepping out onto the playground he felt as if a heavy weight had been lifted from him. Dancing a funny jig he joined the other footballers, but somehow couldn't concentrate on the game. He was relieved when Patsy came over and asked him to go with her to the staff room to take back the teacher's empty mug. He desperately wanted to tell her what he had just done. Patsy was good for things like that. He would never tell Ben or Jamil if he did something good, but Patsy seemed to like him when he was kind or well-behaved.

Arriving at the staff room they found it empty and walked in placing the mug on the sink.

"Never been in here before," said Archie, looking round in interest.

"I have once," said Patsy. "When there was nowhere else free for my clarinet lesson."

For a few minutes they looked round, reading the notices and flicking through a collection of children's books that were lying on the coffee table.

"We should go," said Patsy. "We'll be in trouble if we get caught in here."

They were just about to leave when they heard footsteps coming closer along the corridor. In a moment of panic Patsy hissed, "Quickly hide!"

Both of them dived for cover under a desk in the corner covered with a long cloth. They made it just in time. The footsteps turned in at the staff room door and noises suggested that the owner was making a drink.

Under the desk Patsy looked at Archie obviously terrified.

"What do we do now?" she mouthed silently.

Archie had no idea, but mouthed back, "Keep still, don't make a sound and …" He put his hands together, lifted his head up and shut his eyes, pretending to pray.

After some clanking, which Archie assumed was the stirring of a drink; the footsteps walked over to the desk and stopped.

The owner seemed to be looking at something on the shelves above the desk and, from the black open-toed shoe showing under the cloth, Archie knew who it was.

"Miss Bingham!" he mouthed twisting his face into an agonised expression. Patsy went white and looked like she was going to cry. Archie stopped her with a warning glare.

Both remained perfectly still. Patsy, because she had never been in trouble in her life and didn't intend to start now; and Archie because he couldn't believe that he had just apologised to Mrs Dimple and now here he was, five centimetres from even bigger trouble!

The toe moved closer. Miss Bingham was obviously reaching for something on a high shelf.

"Two more centimetres and she'll stand on my fingers," thought Archie, not daring to move but preparing to stop himself from screaming.

He was saved by the sound of more footsteps.

"Hiya, Sarah."

It was Mr Scott, the deputy head. "I've just terrified some year one boys!" he laughed. "Should have seen them jump when I caught them hiding in the toilets. I'm sure they really do think that I'm a pirate! Want a drink?"

"No thanks, I've just got one. Can you reach this file for me?"

A man's shoe appeared under the cloth.

"Thanks."

Both feet moved away.

"Are you having a good day?" Mr Scott didn't sound too interested but obviously saw the need for polite conversation.

"Yeah, OK."

"Bet you're a bit disappointed the dreaded Archibald's back!"

Under the desk Archie held his breath. Patsy looked at him, screwed up her eyes and grimaced as if she would like to thump Mr Scott.

Miss Bingham waited for a moment before speaking. "You know, I'm not disappointed at all. I'd miss him if he wasn't here."

"Ha, ha, good joke," laughed Mr Scott. "No one would miss him, a pain in the neck, that's what I call him, not a good bone in his body!"

There was silence again before Miss Bingham spoke. This time she sounded rather strange, as if she were furious about something and was carefully controlling her voice.

"Mr Scott," she said slowly, "I happen to think that Archibald Edwards is a fantastic boy. He's worked very hard this term, he has helped me settle into my new school and I like him. In fact …" she paused, "if I ever have a little boy of my own, I hope that he is just like him!"

With that she walked out of the room, followed by Mr Scott apologising in a rather pathetic manner.

Under the desk Archie didn't move. He looked inquiringly at Patsy.

"Did I hear right?" he whispered with such a comical expression on his face that Patsy started to giggle.

"Yes, you did," she looked genuinely pleased. "But come on, let's escape!"

They fled down the corridor and back outside. Archie didn't go straight back to football, he wanted time to think.

"Just like him, just like him …" he repeated to himself.

A warm feeling ran through his body. Miss Bingham would like a little boy 'just like him'. He had been quite bad last week, Miss Bingham knew all about it, but she still wanted a boy like him.

"She likes me," he whispered. "She really, really likes me!"

He danced back to the footballers.

Archie told his Mum about his day when she was sitting on the edge of his bed that night.

"It's so strange," he said, his eyebrows furrowing into a quizzical position.

"Miss Bingham knows that I always get in trouble, she knows that I was bad the day she was away and that Mrs Dimple always says I'm naughty … but she still likes me! And she said it to Mr Scott when I was under the table, so she didn't know I was listening … so she couldn't have been lying! It's like she has completely forgotten what I've done!"

Mum laughed at the outburst and reached over to the bookcase on the opposite side of the bed. She pulled out a Bible and opened it.

"Let me read you something, Archie," she said thumbing through the pages.

"It says in here that 'God shows his love for us in that while we were still doing lots of things wrong Jesus died for us.' And another verse says, 'I will remember your wrong things no more.' You know, Archie, Miss Bingham is showing you a lot about God."

"Is she?" Archie hadn't heard Miss Bingham even mention God, apart from in the end of the day prayer.

Mum continued. "Miss Bingham likes you just the way you are, even though you're not perfect. And Archie, God loves you and likes you, even though he knows everything about you including your thoughts."

Archie turned his head away so his Mum couldn't see him blush!

"Miss Bingham knows you were sorry for being naughty, and that you apologised to Mrs Dimple, and she has forgiven you and decided not to keep bringing up what you did. She's given you a fresh start. In the same way, God wants to forgive you too, Archie. The Bible says that if you are really sorry you can ask God to forgive you and He will wipe all the wrong things away and give you a new start, as if you had never done anything wrong!"

"Wow!" said Archie. "And no punishment either?"

"No," said Mum gently. "No punishment because Jesus has already been punished instead of you when He died on the cross. Think about it, Archie."

She kissed him goodnight and left him deep in thought. He knew he did lots of things wrong and sometimes he felt really bad about it.

"Sorry God," he whispered into the silence. "Please give me a new start and thank you very much that Jesus was punished instead of me! Amen!"

That night Archie had a dream. For some reason Miss Bingham and Mr Scott got married and they were expecting a baby. Miss Bingham got bigger and bigger until eventually she popped! In the next scene the proud parents were waiting in a hospital room when a nurse appeared with a wrapped up little bundle. Slowly the nurse pulled back the covers announcing, "This is your son!"

Mr Scott let out an excruciating scream and ran out of the room. But Miss Bingham smiled dreamily and said, "Oh good, it's just like him."

There, beaming out of the blankets, with a bright red nose and a dummy in his mouth, was a miniature Archie!

## Chapter 9

# ROCK OR REINDEER?

I t was now the start of November. Half-term had passed quickly but for the first time ever Archie had looked forward to going back to school after the holiday. The overheard conversation in the staff room had made a big difference to Archie. He was quite determined that Miss Bingham should continue to like him and although he had lost none of his spark, liveliness and enthusiasm, he had basically been well-behaved.

There was just one cloud on the horizon and that seemed to be drawing nearer with increasing speed. The Christmas play! Each year the infants performed a simple Nativity play; year three organised the carol service; and years five and six produced a play in the summer, which left year four, who annually performed some kind of show with a Christmas theme.

Many of the children enjoyed the practices for the plays with all the singing and dancing and skiving off lessons. For Archie, however, the last few years had been disastrous!

When he was in the reception class Archie had been given the role of a king, alongside Ben and Jamil. He had been proud of himself in his bright red robe and golden crown, even though he overheard Mrs Dimple telling someone that they were only given those parts so they would have to sit at the back of the hall for most of the play and not be seen! All they had to do was walk down the aisle carrying a present, bow to baby Jesus and say loudly, "I bring a present for the King."

Practices had all gone well and during the actual show Ben and Jamil had bowed superbly and said, "I bring a present for the King," in such clear, resounding voices that everyone clapped. When it was Archie's turn, he too bowed low but then announced extremely loudly, "I need a wee!"

The audience roared with laughter. Mrs Dimple whispered sharply, "You're meant to say 'I bring a present.'"

To which Archie replied loudly, "I know I'm meant to say 'I bring a present', but I need a wee first." He ran out of the hall and returned from the toilet with his robe tucked in his trousers.

After that Archie had been banned from ever having a speaking role in a play again.

In year one he had been allowed to be a sheep with seven other boys. The play itself was 45 minutes long and the sheep had to crawl onto the stage, say "baa, baa" four times and crawl off again. Jamil calculated that it took precisely thirty-two seconds if they did it slowly. After weeks and weeks of

practice Archie was eventually banned from baa-ing in the actual performance when Mrs Dimple overheard him telling Patsy that he actually intended to boing onto the stage like a frog and say "moo".

In year two the teachers thought they had found him an ideal part. He was to be the rock that baby Jesus' manger rested on. The idea was that, as he was on his own, he would have no one to talk to; he wouldn't be seen as he would have a grey sheet over him; and he would have to keep still and not fidget as the manger would be balanced on his back!

Again, all had gone well until the real performance when Archie developed a severe case of hiccups, meaning baby Jesus jumped up and down throughout the night. Worse than that, in the final scene, as the kings bowed down to worship, Archie did the most amazing sneeze, catapulting baby Jesus over the kings' heads and on to Mrs Dimple's knee.

\*　\*　\*

"What are they going to make me be this year?" he solemnly asked Ben and Jamil as they waited for the bell.

"Well, you certainly won't be a rock!" sniggered Jamil. They all started to laugh as Patsy came up and joined in.

"Even my Dad said it was the funniest thing he'd ever seen," she giggled.

The bell rang.

Sitting in his place Archie felt nervous. He knew the teachers would have reported all his previous performances to Miss Bingham and, although he thought she would see the funny side, he wasn't sure.

"OK, all of you," said Miss Bingham looking round. "I know all of you want to know about the play. I've written the play this year and it's about what Christmas means to different people in this country. For some of us Christmas is a time for friends and family; for others it's about snow and presents; for others trees or decorations and for others it's about the birth of Jesus. There is going to be lots of singing and dancing, jokes and raps. I want you all to enjoy it. I've got a list of parts here."

She stuck a large piece of paper up on the wall.

*Reporter 1*

*Reporter 2*

*Family 1—4 parts*

*Family 2—5 parts*

*Christmas tree*

*Toys x3*

*Snowmen x4*

*Snowflakes x6—dance*

*Father Christmas*

*Reindeer x2*

*Mary*

*Joseph*

Everyone read down it.

"Now," Miss Bingham continued, "I have ideas for some parts. Ben, having watched you and Jamil rapping in the playground I'd like you to be Father Christmas for me, with Jamil and Lucy as your reindeer—Lucy's a good dancer and she has a lovely voice."

Miss Bingham went down the list giving out parts and discussing what each role entailed. Archie hadn't spotted anything on the list that could be him. He had wondered if he could possibly be a mound of snow, with a white sheet over him instead of last year's grey. He had also wondered about being a present under the tree. He was just imagining how during the finale he could jump out and shout, "Boo!" when Miss Bingham brought him back into the real world.

"Archie, I want you and Patsy to take the parts of the two reporters. In a way they are the main parts as they speak in between scenes and hold the whole play together."

Archie was struck dumb, Jamil pretended to faint and Henrietta's hand shot up.

"W ... w ... w ... will ... Will I have to speak, Miss?" Archie stammered.

Ben nudged him, "You sound like me!" he hissed.

"Oh course you'll have to speak, you're a reporter, that's what they do," said Miss Bingham, amused by his reaction.

Henrietta could resist no longer.

"But he can't, Miss! He's banned!" she shouted in triumph.

"Henrietta," rebuked Miss Bingham. "You know I don't like people telling tales. I've spoken to Mrs Dimple and she is quite happy for Archie to be a reporter."

The ring of untruth in her voice seemed to have gone unnoticed by most of the class, but Archie had heard it clearly.

At lunchtime he waited behind.

"Miss Bingham, is Mrs Dimple really happy for me to be a reporter?" he asked, hoping that she would tell him the truth.

"Well, Archie …"

"That means no," he thought, noticing her pause.

"What Mrs Dimple actually said was that I'm totally mad to choose you and I would live to regret it. However, she did say that it was my play and I could do whatever I liked... and I want you and Patsy to be the reporters."

"But Miss, I don't know if I can do it."

"Archie, I know you can." Miss Bingham sat on the desk so her eyes were level with his. "You're just what we need to hold everything together. You're funny, expressive, have a lovely loud voice and you'll be totally great. Please do it for me Archie, I can't think of anyone better."

Put like that, Archie couldn't refuse.

"Brilliant at poems, brilliant at maths and now a main part," he said, grinning. "What will Mum and Dad say about this one?"

# Chapter 10

# ON TV?

It was hard to be enthusiastic about a Christmas play when Bonfire Night had only just gone by. Archie practiced his lines in the bath, at the tea table, in fact everywhere, and by the end of November even his little sister Molly knew the first two scenes by heart.

The appearance of trees, lights and decorations in the shops made Christmas begin to approach more quickly. It was, however, an announcement by Miss Bingham that made the play practices suddenly take on a new urgency.

It was after dinner on the first Tuesday in December that Miss Bingham said she had some important news to tell the class.

"I've had a phone call during lunchtime," she announced. "A while ago I sent the script for our Christmas play to the national television studios as part of a competition. The organisers have looked at scripts sent in by primary schools from all over the country and chosen four schools to invite to the studios to perform their play. The plays will then be shown on television and people will be asked to phone in to vote for their favourite. The most popular play will win a prize."

She paused, every eye fixed on her.

"Anyway, the phone call was to say that we are one of the four schools chosen to go to the studios."

There was a stunned silence while everyone took in the news.

"So we're going to be on telly, Miss?" Archie broke the silence.

"Yes, Archie, you're all going to be on television and we'll have to get everyone we know to vote for us!"

Suddenly the class exploded, everyone talking and laughing, excited at the prospect. Only Archie remained subdued.

"What is it, Archie?" asked Miss Bingham sidling quietly over to his place.

"I'm just thinking what it will be like when I do something to spoil this play now," he groaned. "You know about the

wee, the mooing frog, the hiccups and the sneeze ... what if I do something terrible this time ... everyone in the world will see me!"

"Archie, I knew when I picked you there was a chance we would be on TV." Miss Bingham explained. "I picked you because I thought you'd be the best at it whether we were on TV or not."

"But what if I mess it up for everyone?"

"You won't."

Archie wasn't too sure.

Everyone ran out of school that evening frantic to be the first to announce the news. Jamil was the most enthusiastic, shouting louder than everyone, "Hey Mum, I'm going to be a famous rapping reindeer on TV!"

His Mum looked at him as if he was mad, but as everyone else came out shouting equally silly things she decided that she'd better listen.

Archie told his Mum the news quietly and was strangely silent as they drove home.

"What's the matter, love?" she asked as they sat at the kitchen table with Molly conveniently playing outside.

"Oh I don't know," Archie blurted out, with his elbows on the table and his head in his hands. "It's just I do want to be on TV, and I do want to be the main part, but I know I'll do something silly. Everyone always laughs at me and I always get everything wrong and I know I'll do something stupid in this play and spoil it for the whole class!"

Mum smiled at him. "Archie, never forget that God made you," she said gently. "He has given you lots of fantastic gifts and making people laugh is one of the most wonderful things you can ever do. Never, ever try to stop being who you are.

## Archie!—TV Star

You go to those studios and do your very best and, even if everything goes totally wrong, you'll have tried your hardest and me and Dad will be very proud of you."

"Me proud too!" Molly's voice announced enthusiastically from the doorway. "Archie a film star!"

"But what if it all goes wrong? What if I forget all my lines? What if I faint or I'm sick?"

"Just do your best, Archie," said his Mum. "That's all anyone can ask!"

## Chapter 11

# STAGE FRIGHT

Jamil calculated that there were precisely two weeks, two days and 45 minutes between Miss Bingham's announcement that they were to be on TV and the arrival of year four at the television studios. Most of those two weeks and two days had been spent rehearsing and re-rehearsing; making costumes and props or, in Archie's case, panicking.

Now sitting beside Ben with a bucket between his knees feeling exceptionally sick, Archie was praying that the bus would break down or even crash! He kept repeating the verse his Mum had read to him from the Bible the previous evening.

'Do not be afraid; the Lord your God will be with you wherever you go.'

"So Archie," she had said gently, "Don't worry about tomorrow. When you are standing in the TV studio remember that God is right there beside you. He will be with you no matter what happens."

Archie glanced round wishing that it was sometimes possible to see God. It would be so much easier to feel better if God was sitting next to him, holding his hand.

Arriving at the studios, the children were greeted by a trendily dressed young man.

"Hi folks," he said jovially. "My name's Alex. Felicity, the producer of your show, sent me down to you. I'm going to show you to your dressing rooms and then give you a quick tour of the studios. Grab your things and follow me!"

They were shown into six small dressing rooms and, having organized all the props and costumes, they obediently followed Alex.

"Are you not leaving that bucket behind?" Alex asked Archie, who was still hugging it to himself like a favourite teddy bear.

"He thinks he might be sick," Jamil butted in. "He's not had too much luck with Christmas plays in the past."

A few people giggled.

"Stage fright," said Alex. "Once you're on stage you'll forget all about it. Seen it loads of times."

The tour round the studios was fascinating. Alex showed them the sets of various popular children's programmes; explained about the sound and lighting equipment and even allowed them to sit in the newsreader's chair.

After half an hour he stopped outside studio five, and dramatically announced, "This is it folks. The moment you've all been waiting for. Buckets at the ready, this is your recording studio!"

Stepping inside Archie wasn't sure if it was nervousness or

excitement he felt. He certainly felt a surge of something that left him desperately needing the toilet.

"I want all of you to come up the steps onto the stage," Alex continued. "I want you all to get a feel of what it will be like this afternoon."

The first thing that struck Archie was how huge the stage seemed compared to the one in their school hall. The second thing was how many seats there were in the audience.

"How many millions are gonna be watching us?" he asked.

Alex laughed. "It looks as if more people can fit in here than actually do," he said. "Anyway you'll not see any of them. Watch this!"

He signalled to some invisible person who, although Archie couldn't see, was obviously there as suddenly the stage was immersed in bright light.

"Look out into the audience now," instructed Alex. "You won't see a lot!"

Archie dropped his bucket and walked to the front of the stage peering forward. Alex was right. Archie could see nothing beyond the edge of the stage.

It was as Archie moved back to his place that a door leading on to the stage burst open and a huge lady with bright yellow, curly hair and very red lips appeared!

"Hello all you lovelies," she exclaimed dramatically in a high pitched, posh voice. "How is Umpton Primary School today? I am Felicity Pankhurst, the producer of your show!"

She ran towards the children not noticing Archie's bucket

lying on its side on the floor. In a flash her foot became entwined with its handle and Archie watched in horror as she overbalanced, catapulting with increasing speed towards everyone.

Archie lurched to one side just in time, leaving Felicity no option but to grab hold of the two nearest objects to steady her. Ben and Jamil screeched as she firmly gripped their hair.

"Which idiot left that bucket there?" she screamed angrily.

Archie looked guilty and opened his mouth to speak but closed it again quickly having received a glare from Miss Bingham.

Felicity recovered quickly and removed the bucket which seemed to be securely wedged on her large, black boot. Turning round she spotted Archie.

"You there," she said. "What's your name?"

"Archie, Miss. Archibald Edwards."

"Archie!"

She threw her arms round him and pulled his nose into her huge chest.

"You are adorable!"

She held him at arm's length, planted an enormous kiss on each cheek and then turned to go.

"Well good luck everyone!" she exclaimed. "And may the best school win. See you later. Byeeee!"

With that she bustled out of the room, leaving Archie rooted to the spot.

The door shut and everyone began to giggle.

"Oh isn't he adorable," mimicked Jamil, in an accent identical to Felicity's. "Don't we all just love him with his pink lip tattoos on both cheeks?"

Archie blushed scarlet.

"Looks like you've got chickenpox again," mumbled Ben.

"I hope it comes off better than last time," said Archie looking horrified. "I can't appear on TV like this!"

The morning was spent running through the play on the stage. It was quite different having so much room to spread out into but, by the time the children were lined up in costumes ready for the actual performance, they all felt nervous but confident.

As the introductory music played Patsy and a well-scrubbed Archie moved into their starting positions ready to begin. The music stopped. There was silence.

Archie's mouth was dry, his mind blank. Patsy nudged him. "Speak," she hissed.

Archie opened his mouth. He shut it again. He couldn't remember anything! How he wished he were a pile of snow!

Patsy nudged him again.

"Good evening …" she whispered, telling him his first line.
Archie swallowed hard and spoke in a squeak.

"Good evening and welcome to the Umpton TV studio."
He swallowed again and spoke in a stronger voice.

"Today we report to you what Christmas means to the
people in our town."

"Yes, today we report …" Patsy continued.

And suddenly Archie forgot to be nervous, forgot the
audience, and became totally caught up in the action on stage.

It was Ben, Jamil and
Lucy who got the biggest
laugh. They had worked
out a silly reindeer dance
that ended with Jamil
and Lucy kneeling on
one knee while Father
Christmas jumped and
landed lying across them
both. Unfortunately Ben
got rather carried away
and dived with too much
enthusiasm, landing heavily on Jamil who collapsed under his
weight! Ben rolled onto the floor but was unable to get up due
to all his stuffing!

There was a moment's pause until Archie leapt forward.

"Superhero reporter to the rescue," he shouted, lifting Ben to
his feet.

He and Jamil then did the dance they always did when they'd scored a goal in football; Lucy did a few extra cartwheels and the audience cheered as if they'd seen a well-practiced, very funny part of the show!

It was towards the end of the performance that Patsy elbowed Archie and hissed "For goodness sake stop scratching!" in his ear.

Archie hadn't noticed that he had been doing anything unusual, but now he realised just how uncomfortable he felt. His body was beginning to pour with sweat and every bit of him itched intensely!

While the attention of the audience was fixed on six dancing snowmen, he whispered to Patsy out of the corner of his mouth.

"It's that daft Felicity! She must have the same lipstick as me Mum. I'm getting a rash!"

Patsy turned and looked at him.

"You don't look very well," she said in a concerned voice.

"I don't feel very well," replied Archie wishing he had dared to rescue his bucket earlier.

With every approaching second Archie felt worse.

"Keep going Archie," he muttered to himself. "It's nearly over. Not long to go." His head was spinning, he felt very dizzy.

Patsy's loud voice seemed to echo round and round in his head.
"So thank you for joining us for the Christmas news."
Archie mustered every last bit of energy.
"So now it's good night from me …"
"… and it's good night from him," Patsy concluded.

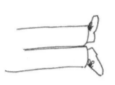 Right on cue, as if it were some great, well-practiced finale, Archie keeled over backwards and fainted. If he had practiced the faint a million times he could not have timed it better. The audience, obviously thinking it was part of the show, clapped and cheered vigorously.

As the rest of the class formed a line and walked to the front of the stage for the final bow, Alex and Miss Bingham secretly carried Archie back to the changing rooms.

"I'm sorry," he muttered. "I knew I'd let you down."

Miss Bingham shoved his head between his knees.

"You didn't let me down, Archie," she said softly. "You were an absolute star!"

*    *    *

In bed that night, covered in cream from head to toe, Archie mulled over the day's events. Despite everything, he had thoroughly enjoyed the day, but at the same time he was dreading the programme being shown on TV the following week.

"The whole country will watch me faint!" he mumbled as his Mum gently stroked his head.

"Don't worry," she reassured him. "Miss Bingham said you were brilliant and very brave."

Archie shut his tired eyes and drifted off to sleep. Slowly his thoughts mingled together into a blur of rashy reindeer, mooing frogs and fainting snowmen. High above them twinkling down from the sky was Archie! A voice echoed all around.

"You're a star, Archibald Edwards ... a star ... a star ... a star!" He fell asleep.

# Chapter 12

# DISAPPEARED!

rchie's mum looked embarrassed and was frowning in an unusually ferocious manner. Sitting cross-legged on the floor of the packed school hall Archie knew that his broken, yellow, plastic bucket, positioned in front of him, was to blame!

Feeling nervous about his appearance on television later that day, Archie had secretly smuggled the bucket out of the shed that morning, just in case he needed to be sick. He knew his Mum would be cross and did feel rather guilty, especially as she had made him his favourite breakfast and been particularly nice to him that morning.

"Remember we will be proud of you no matter what happens, Archie," she had said.

"But Mum," Archie had protested. "I'm going to look so silly. I'll be squeaking and scratching and fainting. Everyone will laugh at me."

"Archie," Mum interrupted. "I've been praying that it will be OK. Let's just see what happens."

Archie had decided that if God could do all the amazing things in the Bible then maybe there was a chance he could get him out of this embarrassing situation; but he still felt so ill that he decided to take his bucket just in case.

On arrival at school Ben had immediately pointed out that

a bucket with three holes and a large crack in the side was a stupid choice for catching sick. Jamil had helpfully calculated where people needed to be positioned around the bucket if they were to be sprayed through the holes if Archie actually did vomit!

Jamil had just nudged Archie to point out that Patsy's dad and Henrietta McTell-Tale were both in the direct firing line, when Mrs Dimple demanded silence.

For three consecutive days the plays from the other schools in the competition had been shown on television. Today parents had been invited into Umpton School to watch their performance together. A huge screen had been erected at the front of the hall and the air was buzzing with excitement. Telephone voting was to begin as soon as the numbers were given out at the end of Umpton's show and parents were already poised with their mobiles ready. Voting would continue throughout the night and the results were to be announced the following day.

The music began. Archie's heart began to race. Then suddenly there he was, standing with Patsy and speaking in his squeaky voice.

The atmosphere in the hall was electric. Everyone clapped and cheered for every tiny thing that happened and when Archie did his superhero act to save Father Christmas even Mrs

## Archie!—TV Star

Dimple leapt up, punched her fist high in the air, wiggled her hips and shouted, "Go Archie! Go Archie!"

Patsy and Archie remained on stage for the whole play and, although the camera only homed in on them between scenes, they could both be seen in the background in the majority of the shots. Archie's eyes were fixed on himself, ignoring all the main action that everyone else in the hall was watching. He was obviously becoming more and more uncomfortable as the play progressed. Then suddenly, as the TV showed Sarah Jane saying clearly,  "My favourite part about Christmas is remembering Jesus' birthday," Archie gasped, "Oh no," so loudly that everyone turned momentarily to stare at him.

Jamil prodded him in the ribs.

"What d'you say that for?" he asked looking puzzled.

Archie pulled a face.

"Did you not just see what I saw?" he whispered.

Jamil shook his head.

"I just scratched my bottom on national television," Archie groaned. "And look at me now, Jamil, I'm scratching up my nose!"

Sure enough Archie was scratching everywhere and, as the

cameras moved in on them for the final two lines, his face appeared very red and blotchy.

"So it's good night from me …"

"… and it's good night from him!"

Then suddenly on the big screen Patsy was standing alone and a gasp went up from Joshua, the youngest boy in the school.

"He's disappeared!"

Another infant joined in.

"Archie must be magic!"

With that, every child in the lower years turned round, craning their necks to try to get a glimpse of the amazing boy who came to their school and that was that. In six short words Archie had moved from 'ill Archie the schoolboy fainter' to 'amazing Archie the great magician'.

"How did you get away with that one?" mouthed Ben.

Archie shrugged his shoulders.

"That's what comes with being a superhero," he said modestly.

As Archie walked out of school that evening, little Joshua sidled up to him.

"Archie, will you come and do magic at my party?" he asked shyly, gazing up at him in admiration. Archie looked down at him, amused.

"I might do," he said. "If I'm not too busy saving the world!"

# Chapter 13

# WHERE'S HE GONE?

There were five minutes to go before the announcement of the results. The hall was again packed with anxious parents, some still ringing or texting Umpton County Primary School's voting number to the studios.

A film crew was positioned in each school to record the children's reactions as the results were given out.

Mrs Dimple called for silence.

The voice on the TV began to speak.

"We can now tell you which of the four schools have received the fewest votes and are therefore out of the competition."

Silence.

"In no particular order, the two schools that have done very well but are out of the competition are …"

Everyone held their breath.

"Compton County Primary School and Saint Hilda's Church of England School."

Pictures from the two schools appeared on screen showing lots of children with disappointed faces. Meanwhile in Umpton's hall, after the initial cheer, there wasn't a sound to be heard as everyone held their breath and waited.

"So," the voice continued, "We have two schools left in the competition: Umpton County Primary with 'Reports about

Christmas' and Crossways County Primary School with 'Christmas Rocks'.

"And the winner of this year's Christmas play award is …"

Archie's voice broke the silence. "Get on with it!"

Everyone laughed.

"Umpton County Primary with 'Reports about Christmas'."

Everyone was on their feet making whooping sounds, jumping up and down and generally going wild. Archie joined in for a moment and then spotted something through the crowd of children that filled him with horror. A side door in

the hall had opened and, unknown to the rest of the celebrating children, a large yellow-haired lady had crept in.

"Well done, all you darlings!"

Felicity Pankhurst's resounding voice split the air. She breezed down to the front, oblivious of children crying as she squashed their fingers beneath her incredibly big feet.

"Now where is my little Archie?" she asked, making all year three snigger.

"Will you, my lovely little treasure, and Patsy Primrose please come to the front."

Patsy moved forward.

# Archie!—TV Star

Mrs Dimple stood up. "Archibald Edwards, Ms Pankhurst wants you!" she declared, peering round.

Archie was nowhere to be seen.

"He's disappeared again!" shouted Joshua.

Gasps of "Wow!" and "I'm having him for my party," filled the air.

Mrs Dimple looked cross.

"Jamil, come here instead," she ordered. Jamil pulled a face and moved forward very slowly.

Felicity Pankhurst continued, "I have the great pleasure of presenting this cheque for £10, ooo, a free outdoor activity holiday for year four and this trophy to Umpton County Primary School for being the winners of this year's Christmas play award!"

Everyone clapped. Ms Pankhurst kissed Patsy on each cheek and eventually managed to land one on the end of Jamil's nose as he dodged from side to side.

"Now, is there anything you'd like to say?" beamed Ms Pankhurst, obviously waiting for a compliment.

Patsy obliged and gave a lovely thank you speech that Mrs Dimple had made her learn just in case they won. She finished and the cameras turned to Jamil. He cleared his throat.

"Before I begin," he said grandly. "Can I just say hello to my mum, my dad, my two sisters and four brothers; my three uncles, four aunties and 12 cousins; my grandparents and their dog, cat and pig; my other grandparents and their pet snake called slippery Sid; my next-door neighbours and their pet parrot who can now actually say my name instead of calling me Jamily Dodger; my best friends …"

Mrs Dimple stuck her head round the side of the camera, giving the impression on screen that Jamil had had his head replaced with hers.

"Jamil, I think that's quite enough hellos for one day," she said, obviously displeased. "I would like to thank everyone for their help and support, especially Ms Pankhurst."

A bouquet of roses was thrust into Jamil's hands, and, holding them at arm's length, he passed them on to Ms Pankhurst. She hurriedly took one more glance around for her favourite boy before leaving the hall with the rest of the film crew.

It was only then, when she was certain they had definitely gone, that Miss Bingham carefully and quietly opened the PE cupboard door and Archie crept out.

"Thank you, Miss," he sighed. "You saved my life!"

## Chapter 14

# TERRY THE TARANTULA

Lying on his bed, listening to the occasional passing car, Archie was trying to work out what to do. He supposed it was the middle of the night as he couldn't hear any movements in the house apart from Dad's occasional snores! Tomorrow was the last day of term and Archie had kept meaning to ask his Mum to buy a Christmas present to give to Miss Bingham.

Archie had never given a teacher a present before, but somehow this year it seemed important. Archie knew he had changed during the term and he knew a lot of that was due to Miss Bingham. It had been in Sunday school the previous week that he had decided he would like to get her a present. Johnny had been telling them a story about ten people who were healed by Jesus. Apparently only one of them remembered to say 'thank you'.

Johnny had looked at each one of them in turn and asked, "I wonder if there is anyone you should say thank you to?"

Archie could think of loads of people but it was Miss Bingham that stood out. The problem was that he had completely forgotten to mention it to his Mum and now it was too late.

He looked round his room, lit dimly by a street lamp outside his window, a plan was slowly forming in his head. He lay for a moment, trying to push a niggling doubt about the idea out of his mind. Then he jumped out of bed, climbed on a chair and unhooked a piece of elastic dangling from the ceiling. Flicking on his lamp he gazed at the furry object in his hand.

"Hello Terry," he whispered, stroking it gently.

He had bought the spider about a year ago, spending all his birthday money to buy the most realistic model tarantula he could find! This one covered his whole hand and was so lifelike that it had terrified not only his entire family, but also every visitor that had entered the house for five months. It was now about seven months since Archie had taken the joke a bit too far.

Mr and Mrs Jensen from up the road had called in for a cup of coffee with his Mum. Mr Jensen was a small, thin, weak looking man and his wife was at least 10 times bigger than him in every way! After two hours of entertaining Molly in the garden, Archie was bored. Unseen, he tiptoed into his room and carried 'Terry' downstairs. He waited and, just as Mrs Jensen started a new story about her arthritic shoulder, he launched him into the air. As 'Terry the tarantula' landed on her arm Mrs Jensen screamed and leapt higher than a pole-vaulter, landing heavily  on Mr Jensen's knee. He screamed even louder and when the ambulance arrived it turned out that he had two broken legs!

Terry had been tied to a piece of elastic and banned from ever leaving Archie's bedroom again.

Looking down at Terry, Archie convinced himself that his idea was a good one.

"Surely," he thought. "If she likes caterpillars, she'll love tarantulas."

He found a piece of paper and undid Terry from the elastic. He felt rather sad.

"Goodbye, Terry," he said solemnly. "Have a good life and I hope I see you again one day."

He wrapped the paper round him and held it in position with the elastic.

\*  \*  \*

Archie arrived at school the next morning with Terry safely in his pocket. He knew his mum must not see.

Sitting in his place, Archie felt pleased with himself. Almost everyone else had a present for Miss Bingham in front of them and he would have felt bad if he had nothing to give.

As soon as Miss Bingham entered the classroom she was swamped with children giving her presents and following registration they all sat on the floor near her desk for a grand opening session.

After lots of candles, chocolates and bubble bath it was, at last, Archie's parcel sitting on her knee.

"That's from me, Miss," Archie announced proudly. "I forgot to put me name on it."

He watched excited. Surely a caterpillar lover, like himself, would like this present better than all the other girly things.

She stretched the elastic and the paper fell open. Luckily Archie missed Miss Bingham's initial reaction due to Henrietta's bloodcurdling scream.

"Help!" she screeched. "It's alive! I don't like spiders!"

She dived to the back of the class. Everyone started to giggle.

"Er, thank you Archie," said Miss Bingham. "It's … er … It's … lovely."

"I knew you'd like it Miss," said Archie triumphantly. "'Cos you like caterpillars like me!"

Miss Bingham smiled and placed it at the far end of her desk whilst she opened her other gifts.

Archie was banned from taking Terry out for a walk in the playground at break so played football instead. After break Miss Bingham had arranged all kinds of Christmas activities for them to do. It was as Archie stuck his last snowflake on to his Christmas card that disaster struck. Mrs Dimple entered the classroom to wish all the children a happy, safe, well-behaved holiday. She opened her mouth to speak but, instead of her well-planned speech, all that came out was a deafening screech. She ran out of the classroom, smashed the glass on the fire alarm and then returned to the classroom screaming at the children to get out.

As the fire bell began to ring, everyone ran terrified through the fire doors and on to the field. As the whole school congregated in their fire drill places, silence was ordered and registers were taken. Everyone was madly sniffing the air and craning their necks to watch for flames.

Two fire engines, lights flashing, sirens wailing, whizzed into the yard, and six firefighters jumped out. Archie was pleased to see his Dad was on duty and waved frantically to get his attention.

In the silence Mrs Dimple could be heard talking to the officer in charge.

"Yes, that's right … I cleared them out immediately. Yes, in year four's classroom."

The firemen disappeared inside.

Jamil lent forward.

"Did you see a fire in our classroom, oh clever, clever Patsy?" he whispered in her ear.

She shook her head.

A murmur ran along year four's line. Everyone agreed that they hadn't noticed anything unusual, not even a whiff of smoke.

A minute later the firefighters reemerged looking amused.

Ben nudged Archie, pointing his finger towards the object that his Dad was carrying. Archie groaned. Dad looked at him and rolled his eyes as Mrs Dimple roared, "Archibald Edwards, come here," just like she always used to do.

"What is this?" she demanded, holding something in the air.

"It's Terry, Miss," Archie replied quickly. "Terry the tarantula. It was a present for Miss Bingham."

"And … " continued Mrs Dimple, more furious than Archie had ever seen her, "Do you realise that I thought it was real and have evacuated the whole school because of it?"

"Yes Miss, sorry Miss," Archie mumbled desperately trying not to look at Ben and Jamil who were laughing helplessly behind her.

A voice came from the front of the reception line.

"Archie!" Joshua shouted. "Archie, quick! Disappear and she won't be able to get you!"

"How I wish I could!" thought Archie, noticing an unusual look in his Dad's eyes.

*   *   *

## Archie!—TV Star

The afternoon was uneventful compared to the morning's happenings. Miss Bingham put Terry in her handbag where he couldn't cause any more trouble.

With ten minutes to go to the end of term Archie was surprised to see his Dad's face at the window. Miss Bingham saw him too and sent Archie to find out what he wanted.

Returning to the classroom Archie had a huge smile spread across his face. From behind his back he pulled a large bouquet of 20 red roses.

"These are for you, Miss," he announced. "I don't think they'll cause as much trouble as Terry!"

"Archie, they are beautiful," she said looking quite overcome. She bent down and whispered something quietly in his ear. Archie grinned and nodded.

* * *

Hanging Terry back on his elastic that night Archie was pleased that Miss Bingham had suggested that he would be better at looking after a tarantula than she would. Archie had promised faithfully that she could borrow him any time she wanted, but he was pleased that for now at least he was back where he belonged.

He had been surprised that he hadn't been in trouble when he arrived home. Dad seemed to see the funny side of everything and Mum felt guilty that she hadn't thought to buy a present for Miss Bingham in the first place.

"It was very kind of you," she had laughed. "It reminds me of the true meaning of Christmas."

"I don't remember there being a tarantula in the stable," Archie had said seriously, thinking he must listen to Johnny more carefully in future if Terry had a starring role in the story.

Mum had rolled her eyes. "I mean that God gave us the precious gift of Jesus," she corrected. "And you gave Miss Bingham something that was very precious to you."

Somehow the idea that Mum thought he had done something that reminded her of Jesus made Archie feel good inside. He might spend a lot of his life getting into trouble, but deep down he wanted to do things right.

"Goodnight, Terry," he called across the room as he climbed into bed. "You don't half get yourself into some trouble without meaning to. In fact, you're just like me!"